Beast Quest®

KARIXA
THE DIAMOND
WARRIOR

BY ADAM BLADE

ORCHARD

VILLAGE

KING
HUGO'S
PALACE

KARIXA'S MIN

WELCOME TO

Beast Quest

Collect the special coins in this book. You will earn one gold coin for every chapter you read.

Once you have finished all the chapters, find out what to do with your gold coins at the back of the book.

With special thanks to Tabitha Jones

For Chloe and Bethany Gater

www.beastquest.co.uk

ORCHARD BOOKS

First published in Great Britain in 2016 by The Watts Publishing Group

1 3 5 7 9 10 8 6 4 2

Text © 2016 Beast Quest Limited.
Cover and inside illustrations by Steve Sims
© Beast Quest Limited 2016

Beast Quest is a registered trademark of Beast Quest Limited
Series created by Beast Quest Limited, London

A CIP catalogue record for this book is available from the British Library.

ISBN 978 1 40834 309 8

Printed and bound by CPI Group (UK) Ltd, Croydon, CR0 4YY

The paper and board used in this book are made from wood from responsible sources

Orchard Books
An imprint of Hachette Children's Group
Part of The Watts Publishing Group Limited
Carmelite House, 50 Victoria Embankment, London EC4Y 0DZ

An Hachette UK Company
www.hachette.co.uk
www.hachettechildrens.co.uk

TRIAL
OF
HEROES

JUNGLE

CORSAIR
ISLAND

CONTENTS

A great battle has just taken place in Avantia. The City was almost destroyed by a raging Beast, and many lives were at risk...

Thankfully, a courageous warrior came to our aid, and peace was restored to the capital. But this warrior was not Tom, nor was it Elenna, for they were across the ocean, fighting bravely on another Quest. Now Avantia has a new champion, laying claim to Tom's title of Master of the Beasts.

And this courageous fighter has an honest claim to that title, which means there is only one thing for it.

Tom must put his title on the line. He and his opponent must complete the Trial of Heroes.

May the bravest warrior win.

Aduro, former wizard to King Hugo

CRASH LANDING

Tom plummeted through empty space, his fist clamped tight about Dray's tunic collar. His head throbbed from where he'd head-butted the brute before dragging them both into the abyss. Tom blinked hard, forcing Dray's broad face into focus. Dark eyes glared back at him from above a crooked broken nose. Dray let out a growl, baring his tombstone teeth in a snarl of animal rage.

Fierce anger boiled inside Tom. How could Amelia be so devious? She'd told Tom Dray was her uncle, when in fact he was a monster, created by the Evil Wizard, Jezrin.

Still groggy, Tom lifted his sword. He brought it down, hilt-first, towards the imposter's skull. Dray thrust his powerful wrists upwards and out, blocking the blow, tearing free of Tom's grip and smashing the sword from his fingers. With a stab of alarm, Tom watched his weapon spin away. He couldn't let Dray escape. He groped for the big man's

shoulder, just missing. Dray swung
his fist.

"Oof!" The blow landed square
in Tom's chest, punching the air
from his lungs and sending him
tumbling head over heels through
the darkness.

Tom's stomach lurched as he spun. He stared into the blackness, looking for Dray, but couldn't see a thing. He struggled, pumping his arms and legs, trying to right himself, but the air gave no resistance, and he didn't even know which way was up any more.

Then a faint light appeared, spiralling towards him at terrifying speed – a pale gash, getting bigger and brighter by the moment.

The next portal, Tom realised. *The final stage of the Trial of Heroes!* Through the jagged rip, he saw a steep, rocky slope scattered with rubble. A shock of adrenaline jolted him. *I'm going way too fast!* Tom twisted, somehow managing to angle his feet towards the portal. He braced himself...

This is going to hurt. A lot.

He landed with a thud, feet-first on loose scree. His ankle buckled, and he tipped forwards, pitching headfirst down the slope...

"Urgh!" Tom skidded on his belly, sharp stones biting his palms and knees, tearing at his clothes. Bare rock at the bottom of the slope raced towards him. Tom threw up his arms to shield his face, dipped his shoulder and rolled. He slammed to a stop on his back.

For a moment he lay stunned, staring up at a wide arch of clear

blue sky. Then the nagging throb
of countless scrapes and bruises
brought him back to his senses.

Tom heaved himself over and
spotted his sword, just out of reach.

He tried to rise, but a white-hot
pain flared in his ankle and he
sank back to the ground. He gritted
his teeth and reached, pulling his
aching body closer to his weapon.

Crunch! Dray's huge boot came
down on Tom's outstretched wrist,
making him gasp with agony. Tom
struggled to free his hand, but
the huge man was far too heavy.
Dray stooped, lifted Tom's sword
and slowly turned around. Terror
squeezed Tom's chest. His sword

glinted as Dray drew it back ready to strike. With a flash of victory in his pale eyes, Dray brought the blade down.

Thunk! An arrow punched through Dray's thick forearm. Tom's sword hit the ground with a clang, while Dray stared at the hole in his flesh,

his bald forehead creased with confusion. Tom twisted his neck and looked back to see Elenna already fitting another arrow to her bow.

Amelia stood at Elenna's side, glaring at Dray, a huge rock between her hands. Tom blinked in confusion.

"GRAAAH!" Amelia charged forwards with a roar and cannoned shoulder-first into Dray, knocking him sideways. Tom, his arm free, scrambled to his knees to see Amelia smash her rock down on Dray's bald head with a sickening crack. Dray crumpled and hit the ground. He lay still, his eyes closed. Tom couldn't see the big hulk breathing, but that meant nothing. Dray was no mortal

– Tom knew that now.

"Are you all right?" Elenna cried, as she and Amelia rushed to Tom's side. Each held out a hand. Tom took Elenna's, and slowly pulled himself to his feet. He gasped with pain as he put weight on his ankle, but it held. *Not broken!* Tom thought with relief. *Just a sprain.*

"I'm fine," he said. Then he gritted his teeth, and turned on Amelia. "I'm not falling for any more of your tricks!" Tom growled.

Amelia held up her hands. "I'm on your side now!" she said. "I promise! I'm not working for Jezrin any more."

Elenna rolled her eyes. "What? Not now you've been caught, you mean!"

Tom couldn't control his rage. "You should never have been working for him in the first place!" he cried. "You're the descendant of Kara the Fearless – the brave and noble Mistress of the Beasts!"

Amelia looked at her feet. "That's why Jezrin came looking for me," she said, pushing at a stone with her boot. "He told me I was rightful Mistress of the Beasts. He created Dray to be my bodyguard, and gave us a poisoned dart to strike Epos while you were in Gwildor."

Tom shook his head in disgust. "So you could make yourself look like a hero while I looked like a fool?" he said.

Amelia nodded. "The plan was to have you stripped of your title so I could take your place..."

"And when that didn't work, you decided to challenge me for my title instead?" Tom asked.

Amelia kicked the stone away and met Tom's gaze, her cheeks fiery red. "Yes. But now I've worked out that Jezrin was just using me..." She trailed off, and her eyes fell back to the ground.

"There's something more you're not telling me," Tom said.

Amelia tensed. When she finally looked up, her jaw was set, and her blue eyes shone with defiance. "Jezrin wanted me to kill you," Amelia said.

"When you were asleep. But that's a
coward's way. I said no!"

Tom suddenly remembered what
he'd seen in the jungle, and knew

she was telling the truth. "I heard you," he said. "You were arguing with Dray."

Amelia nodded. "Jezrin can talk through Dray. He—"

Elenna gasped and grabbed Tom's sleeve, pointing to the ground where the brute had been lying. "Speaking of Dray," she said, "where is he?"

Tom glanced all around them, and his stomach twisted with dread. Jezrin's murderous creation had gone!

DANGER IN THE MINE

Tom scanned the terrain, looking for Dray. A wide plane of grey rock surrounded them, hemmed in on every side by high cliffs. *A quarry,* Tom realised, *or a mine.* In the distance, he could make out a tall wooden frame built up against the quarry wall, alongside what looked

like the dark openings of caves
or tunnels. But there was no sign
of Dray. Tom gritted his teeth in
frustration. *He's gone!*

"I can't believe we let him escape!"
Amelia said.

Tom looked for a trail, but the
rocky ground held no footprints.
Elenna caught his eye. "I don't like
the idea of leaving Jezrin's thug on
the loose," she said.

Tom frowned, running his eyes
along the steep, barren slopes around
them. "Neither do I," he said. "But
we don't know which way he went.
We'll just have to be on our guard."
Tom pulled the map of the Nowhere
Lands from his pocket and shook
out the folds. Immediately, a glowing
red dot appeared on the parchment.
Tom focused on it, recognising the
contours of the quarry in which they

stood. The dot marked the caves Tom had spotted in the distance. A spidery word was scrawled in golden ink beside it. *KARIXA*.

The final Beast on this Quest...

"That way," Tom said, pointing towards the dark openings.

Tom, Elenna and Amelia made their way over the rocky ground, glancing about as they went. Tom's twisted ankle throbbed with each step, and the sun beat down fiercely on his head and shoulders. Thinking of Dray on the loose and another Beast still to fight, he felt heavy with exhaustion. Daltec had been right. The Trial of Heroes was the ultimate test – four deadly Beasts to face in

order to win the Rune of Courage
and prove himself worthy of the title
of Master. And if he failed, Avantia
would have no Master of the Beasts
to protect it.

*No… I won't give up while my
kingdom needs me.*

Not a single plant or patch of grass
clung to the steep cliffs around them,
but Tom could see deep score marks
where mining tools had scraped
away the rock.

As they drew closer to the caves,
the workings of the mine became
clear. A rickety wooden frame topped
by a metal wheel had been built
against the cliff – a pulley system
to lift ore up to higher ground. A

long, rusted chain hung from the
pulley. Tom shuddered. The ancient,
crooked structure reminded him of a
gallows. Buckets and broken tools lay
scattered on the ground. The mouths
of three tunnels gaped in the quarry
wall. Tom could see ancient, silvered
wood propping up the entrances.

He checked the map again. The red
dot clearly indicated that the Beast
– Karixa – would be found inside
the mine. Tom lifted his eyes to the
largest of the tunnels, wondering
what sort of Beast might lie within.

An orange light flared in the
darkness, then another. Elenna
gasped as torch after torch kindled,
creating a line of bobbing flames

leading away into the mine. Amelia's boots crunched on the grit. She let out a nervous laugh.

"Well, it looks like the final Beast is ready for us!" she said.

Tom nodded. He crossed to the tunnel and stepped inside, with Elenna and Amelia close behind him. The daylight quickly faded as they followed the sloping path downwards. Apart from the echo of their footsteps and the steady drip of hidden water, nothing stirred. Rusted shovels and pickaxes littered the tunnel floor, along with other, more personal items. Tom spotted an abandoned dinner knife, a tarnished cup and even a set of dice. A cold finger traced his spine as he thought of the men that once worked here, eating together, playing games... The discarded items hinted all too well at a horror that had chased the miners out. *If they ever made it out at all.*

"What's that?" Amelia hissed, pointing up ahead. Something large and metallic glinted in the torchlight. As they approached it, sick horror churned Tom's guts. A mass of smooth, twisted metal lay welded to the tunnel floor, blackened in places by soot. In the warped lines of the metal, Tom could make out the unmistakable shapes of a helmet, breastplate and gauntlets, all melded together.

"How horrible," Elenna said. "Do you—"

Tom stopped her with a shake of his head. He didn't want to think about what had become of the owner of that armour.

"Look," Amelia said, pointing to crude marks chiselled on the tunnel wall. Tom quickly saw they were the letters of a verse:

> *Treasure you seek but death you'll find*
> *In the darkness of my mine.*
> *When Karixa walks, your end has come,*
> *Beware the faintest glimpse of sun.*

"It looks like we're on the right track then," Amelia said, her voice too loud in the silence.

Tom shuddered again. "Let's keep going," he said. They followed the line of flickering torches, turning corners and passing the dark openings of smaller tunnels on either side. "I wonder what they mined down here," Tom said, looking at yet another rusted pick abandoned on the ground. "To cut this far into rock, it has to be something valuable."

"I'll say!" Amelia breathed, stopping suddenly as they turned a sharp bend. They had arrived in a large room lit by more torches, with tunnels leading off in all directions. At the far end of the room, a crooked line of closely packed crystals, wider than a door, ran from floor to ceiling. Huge chunks of gleaming stone reflected the torches' orange glow, splintering it into dazzling rainbows.

"Diamonds!" Elenna said.

Amelia was already across the room, running a hand over the jagged, sparkling stones. "Just one of these will feed my whole village for a year!" she said, drawing her axe back to strike the wall.

"No!" Tom cried, sensing danger, but Amelia let her weapon fall.

Clang! A tremendous high-pitched chime rang through the still air. As the sound echoed away, a creaking, crackling started up. Diamonds shifted in the torchlight, coming away from the wall, drawing together, forming a gleaming hand.

"Move!" Tom cried. The hand shot

out and caught hold of Amelia's arm.

"Help!" Amelia tried to tug free but she was trapped. Tom leapt towards her, sword raised to hack at the hand.

"Look out!" Elenna cried, fitting an arrow to her bow. The wall shifted and groaned. A great section of crystals broke away and the huge, shining figure of a woman stepped from the rock. *Karixa!*

The Beast stood even taller than Dray, and twice as wide – made from pure diamond. One of her hands still gripped Amelia, but her other arm ended in a diamond broadsword, honed to a wicked point. She glared about the room, her hollow eyes blazing like fire. Elenna fired her

arrow, but it pinged harmlessly off the Beast's glistening breastplate.

The Beast hurled Amelia aside with a flick of her wrist. Amelia flew across the room, smashing against the far wall and crumpling to the ground. Tom raced towards her, but Karixa crossed the chamber with long strides, easily overtaking him.

She lifted her arm and slapped her hand against Tom's chest, slamming him to the ground. Tom curled into a ball, grimacing with pain. He felt as if each of his ribs had been broken.

A Beast made from indestructible diamond, he thought. *How can we possibly win?*

THE WOUNDED WALL

Tom rolled over and scrambled to his feet, clutching his ribs. The Beast towered over him. The angled surfaces of her broad, chiselled face gleamed in the torchlight and her narrowed eyes shone with a cool blue light of their own. An icy chill ran down Tom's spine as he held Karixa's gaze. He felt like a rabbit cornered by a wolf, wounded and marked to die. He hunkered down into a fighting stance and lifted his sword.

Twang! Elenna's arrow whizzed past him, striking Karixa's shoulder with a chime, before falling to the ground. Karixa's steady gaze didn't leave Tom's face. She slowly lifted her blade. Beyond the Beast, Amelia lay silent on the cold stone, her eyes closed, and one arm twisted beneath her. *Ping!* Another of Elenna's arrows rang harmlessly off the Beast's body. In the shifting torchlight, the stern lines of Karixa's mouth seemed to twitch into a stiff, cruel smile.

"Save your arrows," Tom told

Elenna. "They can't pierce diamond. We need to come up with a different plan." *I just wish I knew what!*

Tom shifted his weight onto his uninjured foot and sprang towards the Beast, brandishing his sword. Karixa lunged to meet his challenge, but instead of striking the Beast's diamond flesh, Tom ducked beneath her blade and raced to Amelia's side. *Crash!* Tom looked back to see Karixa's sword buried in the rock right where he'd been standing.

That blade cuts through rock like a hot knife through butter!

The Beast turned and started to circle, her back hunched in a

panther-like crouch and her eyes
fixed on Tom. She swished her
blade through the air, scattering the
orange light in a dazzling display,
then paced slowly towards him.

"Amelia! Wake up!" Tom cried, shaking her urgently. He felt Amelia stir. She opened her eyes, then lurched to her feet, almost toppling. Tom grabbed her arm to steady her.

"We have to get out of here!" he cried, tugging her towards a tunnel in the wall behind them. Just before he ducked inside, he glanced back to see Karixa striding across the room, still slicing the air with her blade, her eyes glowing bright with amusement. In the shadows behind the Beast, pressed against the chamber wall, Elenna crouched, a single useless arrow aimed at Karixa's back. Tom caught Elenna's eye. She gave a tiny, helpless shrug.

Tom knew there was little Elenna could do to help him. He nodded, and dived into the tunnel with Amelia.

They scrambled together over uneven ground, racing between pools of orange light cast by the torches on the walls. Close behind them, Tom could hear the unhurried footsteps of the Beast gaining steadily. Every step Tom took sent a shock of pain through his ankle. Amelia's axe hung loose in her hand, and she half stumbled as she ran, as if still dizzy.

Crash! The crunch of diamond smashing against rock echoed behind them, making Tom's heart leap in his chest and the torchlight flicker. He glanced over his shoulder to see the Beast hacking great gouges in the tunnel walls. Tom and Amelia hurtled on, the ground shuddering beneath their feet.

Finally, they burst from the tunnel into an open chamber, dimly lit by milky daylight filtering through tiny cracks far above. Uneven bulges and shadowy gashes pitted the walls, showing where thousands of tools had worked the rock. Tom scanned the chamber for any openings, but found only dark, craggy stone, traced through with glittering seams of diamond. He swallowed hard. *No way out.* And he could hear

Karixa right behind them.

"Over there," Tom said, pointing to the far wall, where a mighty overhang cast an inky shadow. He and Amelia sped across the chamber. They threw themselves into the darkness, their backs against the rock. Karixa stepped into the tunnel entrance, filling the opening. Her eyes shone in the half-light, and her transparent body glowed orange from the torchlight behind her. She entered the room, and started to skirt the craggy wall. As she walked, she lifted her deadly sword and dragged the blade across the stone. A hideous grating sound filled the chamber and sparks flew from the tip of her blade.

Fist-sized chunks of rock clattered to the ground.

Tom lifted his sword, which had never felt more useless, and fixed his eyes on the Beast. Beside him, Amelia drew back her axe. A picture flashed through Tom's mind, of the twisted, malformed armour they'd seen near the entrance to the mine. A tremor ran though his body. *How did Karixa melt that armour? She must have hidden powers we've yet to see.*

The Beast let her sword arm drop, and the hideous grating echoed away to silence. Karixa stood tall, her bulky shoulders square and her chin held high as she ran her glowing gaze around the room.

She's knows we're here! Tom thought. *She's just toying with us!*

The Beast's head snapped around as if reading his mind. Her eyes flashed as they fell on Tom and Amelia. Karixa lifted her sword and pointed

ted her blade to meet his attack.
om dived beneath it, drawing back
s sword. *Crash!* He struck the
eakened rock and sprang back
vay from the wall.

Smash! Amelia's axe came down,
ending a boom echoing through the
hamber that rumbled on as great
hunks of rock began to fall. Karixa
urned and swatted her fist at
melia, but Amelia dived away from
he falling wall, and out of the path
f Karixa's blow.

For a heartbeat, everything seemed
 run in slow motion. Karixa's
reat head tipped up, and she froze,
aring at the cascade of rocks
umbling towards her. She lifted her

the sharp tip straight towards Tom's
heart – a message he understood
even without his red jewel.

You won't escape me!

A movement from the tunnel
mouth caught Tom's eye. He glanced

sidelong, barely moving his eyes, to see Elenna slip into the cavern, her bow and arrow raised. She aimed at the Beast's back, scanning Karixa's diamond flesh. *Clink!* Elenna's boot hit a loose stone, sending it skittering across the floor. The Beast turned slowly towards her and Tom's chest tightened in fear.

I have to help Elenna! He studied the wall behind Karixa, laced with cracks, topped with a bulging overhang, and turned to Amelia at his side.

"How strong are you feeling?" he hissed, tipping his head towards the damaged wall. Amelia glanced at the mighty Beast and a flicker

of uncertainty crossed he But then she nodded, her fierce. "Strong enough to oversized ornament!" she s

Tom smiled. "Then let's g

He shot off to the right, a darted left, letting out a ro drew back her axe. The Bea turned towards Amelia, a h glint in her eyes. *Ping!* Ele arrow rang off the Beast's b shoulder, and Karixa's eyes back to Elenna.

Tom drew back his sword he neared the diamond warr focusing on a point behind h the rock where many cracks together. Karixa swung arou

arms, as if to shield her face, then
a cloud of dust and stone engulfed
her, smashing her to the ground and
burying her shining body.

When the groaning and rumbling finally subsided and the air cleared, Tom found himself staring at a mound of broken rock where the Beast had stood. A single shaft of golden sunlight, from a crack high above them, glanced down on the rubble, motes of dust glimmering in its path.

Amelia let out a whoop and punched the air.

"Well, that went better than I'd expected,"Tom said, his voice croaky with dust. "It looks like the last Quest is over."

He heard Elenna gasp, and turned. Tom's heart gave a sickening jolt. Elenna stood, pale and wide-eyed, as

still as a statue. Dray's hulking body
loomed over her, a long knife pressed
to her throat.

"Not quite, Tom," Dray said, his
gruff voice transformed into Jezrin's
unmistakable, evil snarl. "I think
you'll find it's barely begun!"

THE WIZARD'S THREAT

"Let her go!" Tom cried, brandishing his sword and stepping towards Elenna. Dray's scowling face shifted horribly, as if something living were crawling beneath the skin. When the rippling, twitching movements stopped, Dray's broad features had morphed into Jezrin's sharp nose and keen dark eyes.

"It will take more than a few rocks to defeat Karixa," Jezrin sneered. "But defeat her you will. The Rune of Courage is hidden in these caves.

I need it! You will complete your Quest and bring it to me."

"Never!" Tom and Amelia cried together.

Jezrin's lips spread into an evil smile. Beneath his knife, Elenna stiffened. The whites of her eyes showed bright in the gloom.

"No?" Jezrin said. "In that case, your friend will die. And you will never complete the Quest without my assistance. Not even down here, where Karixa is unable to harness the power of the sun. Your puny weapons have no effect on her diamond flesh."

Tom gritted his teeth, his mind racing for a way to get Elenna to safety. It would take only seconds to reach his friend – but that was more than enough time for the Evil Wizard to slit her throat.

"Don't try anything stupid," Jezrin said.

Tom saw Elenna's eyes flash with rage. She drew back her elbow and drove it hard into Dray's gut, but the giant body beneath Jezrin's face didn't even flinch.

Jezrin let out low chuckle. "You see, I—" A deafening roar swallowed the wizard's words and the room trembled.

"Tom!" Amelia shrieked, cannoning into his side, throwing him to the ground. Chunks of rock exploded in all directions from the mound where Karixa lay. Tom buried his head in his arms, fragments of stone pummelling his tunic.

When the clatter of rock had fallen silent, Tom looked up to see sunlight streaming into the chamber from a wide crack in the ceiling. Jezrin still held Elenna, but his sneer had changed to a grimace of terror. Beneath the golden rays, Karixa stood tall, her arms spread wide and her eyes lifted to the light flooding down on her body. Where the golden beams pierced her diamond flesh, the glittering crystal flared bright, filled with rainbow fire. Tom could see the pure energy of the sun reflecting back on itself, trapped inside Karixa's body, building to a bright, pulsing point in her chest.

Finally, when the ball of light in Karixa's chest blazed so bright it hurt Tom's eyes, the Beast let her massive arms fall. She turned slowly, her narrowed eyes burning like molten gold, a huntress seeking prey.

The Beast's smouldering gaze fell on Dray. Elenna screamed as two sizzling golden beams shot from Karixa's eyes, hitting Dray square in the forehead.

For a moment, he shuddered, caught in the shafts of light, then his mouth opened in a silent cry. Elenna scrambled away, and Tom found himself backing off too.

Cracks of light spread across Dray's skin like clay heated too fast in a kiln.

BOOM!

Jezrin's minion exploded, showering everyone with chunks of brittle debris. A cloud of grey dust, lit by slanting shafts of sunlight, billowed up.

Karixa stood beneath the shattered chamber ceiling, her body dim, but starting to brighten as she drew more light into herself.

"Let's go before she recharges!" Amelia cried.

Tom turned from the Beast and scanned the murky room. He spotted Elenna, caked in ashy dust, rising shakily. He raced to her side.

Elenna coughed. "I'm all right," she said.

"That way!" Amelia shouted, pointing towards the tunnel mouth. All three of them dashed into the passage and ran. Soon a brighter, pulsing light shone from behind them and the sound of heavy footsteps almost drowned out their own.

"She's coming!" Tom cried. He sprinted on, ignoring the pain in his ankle, tracing their path back out of the mine. Finally, he could see a bright arch of daylight up ahead, but the light behind them was brighter still as Karixa's footsteps boomed loud in his ears. Tom, Amelia and Elenna burst from the tunnel, and dived behind a boulder. Tom sank into a crouch, gasping for breath, and tightened his grip on his sword. *Maybe out here in the open we'll have a better chance against Karixa.* But as Tom thought of the sun beating down all around them – a source of endless power for the Beast – a sharp stab of fear knifed through his guts.

One way or the other, this will be the end of my trial...

1

5

A BOY WITH A SWORD

Tom peered over the top of the boulder to see Karixa stride from the mouth of the tunnel and out into the open. The sight of her huge, invincible body shining like white fire in the sunlight made Tom gasp. *How are we going to defeat her?* Beside him, Amelia let out a low whistle under her breath.

The diamond warrior spread her arms wide and lifted her eyes. A look of bliss lit her angular features as her body captured the sun's rays. A hideous ticking, like rain falling on hot metal, seemed to come from all around her. The fierce light building inside Karixa's body focused in the depths of her chest, glowing brighter and brighter until Tom had to shield his eyes. Then Karixa lowered her arms, and turned her gaze towards him.

"Get down!" Tom cried, ducking behind the boulder.

Crack! The whole rock exploded, throwing Tom backwards. White

light and the clatter of falling debris filled his senses, along with the choking stench of scorched stone.

His chest tightened at the thought of what that deadly beam would do to human flesh.

"Run!" He cried, scrambling to his feet. He, Elenna and Amelia raced over the rubble-strewn ground and dived behind another boulder in the shadow of the cliff wall. *Crash!* Two

bright bolts of energy lashed the cliff above them, melting rock away.

They kept running, hurtling behind a new rock as a thunderous roar echoed around them. Tom glanced back to see a mound of blackened stone crash to the ground, engulfing their previous hiding place. Karixa opened her arms once more, channelling more sunlight into her body, recharging for another strike.

"We can't just run and hide!" Elenna hissed. "We have to do something."

Tom nodded. "I don't think we can defeat her – our weapons aren't strong enough. But if I distract her, maybe you and Amelia can hunt for the Rune of Courage in the mine. It's the rune we need to complete the Trial of Heroes. It's our only hope."

"But that's crazy," Elenna said. "You can't stand up to her alone – she'll vaporise you with one look!"

"You're not helping!" Tom said.

Amelia shrugged. "Elenna's got a point. We should face the Beast together."

Tom shook his head. "We can't destroy diamond. Our best chance is to find the rune. I'll keep her distracted until you get back. I can't see any other way of completing the Quest."

Elenna looked uneasy, but nodded. "All right," she said. Then she held

Tom's eye for a long moment. "But be careful. No heroics. I expect to find you out here alive."

"I'll do my best," said Tom. "Now, let's go, while the Beast's recharging. On a count of three, make a run for the mine. One... Two... Three!"

Tom sprang from their hiding place, coming out into the open to stand face to face with Karixa. Terror fizzed through his body as he locked eyes with the Beast. Her gaze burned like the white-hot fire right at the heart of a forge. There was no mistaking the grin on her lips. *I'm dead!* Tom thought, anger raging inside him at the stupidity of his own hasty mistake.

Two rays of light shot from Karixa's eyes, converging to a single deadly beam. Tom lifted his sword on instinct, into the path of the dazzling ray.

The energy beam glanced off the flat of Tom's blade and bounced straight back into Karixa's face. The Beast threw her arm before her eyes and reeled back as if she'd been punched.

"Nice swordsmanship, Tom!" Amelia cried, as she and Elenna ran.

Karixa shook her giant head, and slowly unbent. It wouldn't be long before she started to refuel. But now Tom felt alive with new energy and

hope. *She isn't invincible. She can
be stopped!* Tom might not have his
Golden Armour or shield tokens,
but before he'd won any of those he
had been just a boy with a sword. *I
survived then and I'll survive now!*

Not far from where Karixa stood, the wooden mining frame clung crookedly to the cliff wall. A long chain ran up to the pulley wheel at the top of the frame, then down again to a winch drum with a crank handle. The sight of the noose-like hook and chain gave Tom an idea. The pulley had once been used for hauling diamonds up the side of the cliff. *It's about time it was used again.*

"Change of plan! I need you to man the winch!" Tom cried, pointing.

"What are you going to do?" Amelia asked, already racing towards the drum with Elenna.

"Capture the Beast!" Tom said.

He sped towards the rusted chain, grabbed the hook, and tugged. Nothing budged. *It's rusted stiff,* Tom realised, wishing briefly for the strength of his golden breastplate. He banished the thought. *I can do this!* He braced his feet against the ground, took a deep breath and pulled. Again, nothing happened. Tom felt a wave of frustration. He glanced at Karixa, only to see her lift her arms to the sky. Then he clenched his teeth and heaved once more. Suddenly, the pulley wheel screeched, and the chain tumbled downwards with a metallic clatter.

"Watch out!" Elenna cried from her post at the winch.

Tom jumped aside and the chain rippled past him. Soon a pile lay at his feet, still connected at one end to the winch via the pulley wheel. Tom grabbed the hook from the pile, took a length of slack chain in his hands, and started to swing it like a lasso, his eyes on Karixa's glowing form. Tom could feel the weight of the chain tugging at his muscles as the hook gained speed. He could hear the air crackling and sizzling as the Beast recharged, glowing ever brighter.

The Beast lowered her mighty arms. Tom knew he couldn't wait any longer. He drew back his arm and sent the hook flying, letting the rough metal links of the chain flow through his fingers. Karixa turned, her gaze burning... *Clang!* The chain struck her shin and coiled tightly around her leg. She let out a roar of rage.

"Heave!" Tom cried. He dashed to the drum winch that fed the pulley, grabbed the wooden crank handle alongside Amelia and Elenna, braced his back and tugged.

Even with the three of them turning together, Tom had to strain every muscle to shift the handle. The pulley wheel screeched and the chain about Karixa's leg went taut. Karixa lifted her foot, bellowing as she tried to pull it free. But the metal chain was wrapped too tight. She focused her eyes on the metal links, ready to melt them with fire.

"Pull!" Tom cried again. The three of them heaved together.

Karixa lurched sideways and toppled, her leg tugged from under her. Two bolts of bright energy shot from her eyes as she fell, striking the cliff, blasting off a huge chunk of rock. Karixa hit the earth with a crash that jolted Tom's spine. She beat her mighty fist on the ground and let out a howl of rage as Tom, Elenna and Amelia hauled her over the rock.

Tom's arms burned with the strain and he could hear Amelia panting

with each turn of the crank. Elenna's
face was pink and streaked with dust
and sweat. But, slowly, inch by inch,
they lifted the struggling Beast off
the ground and up the cliff. Finally,
Karixa hung high above them, her

diamond body empty of light, but her eyes blazing with fury.

"Hold her steady," Tom told Amelia and Elenna. Then he stepped towards the Beast.

"Karixa!" Tom cried. "You are beaten. Surrender and we'll set you free."

The Beast watched him for a moment, not a flicker of submission in her fierce eyes. Then she twisted her body and swiped her sword-arm up at the chain. She missed, and swiped again, but her sword arm wouldn't reach.

"Surrender," Tom said again. "You are trapped."

Karixa shot him a look of defiant

rage. Her lips twitched into a furious smile. She twisted once more, and swung her sword. A deafening note, pure and terrible, rang out across the quarry as diamond blade sliced diamond flesh.

She's cut off her own foot!

Karixa fell, turning a tight somersault in the air, and landed in a one-kneed battle crouch.

RETURN TO DARKNESS

Karixa lunged, her movement unbalanced and awkward, but her eyes burning with rage.

"Back into the mine!" Tom cried, pointing to the nearest tunnel. It was pitch black inside, but suddenly, a torch flared in the darkness. Tom sped towards the

tunnel mouth with Amelia and
Elenna at his side. They dived into
the shadowy refuge and ran. Torches
flared around them, lighting their
way as they went.

The passageway bore deep into
the cliff, a long, straight tunnel
without branches or turns. Tom,
Elenna and Amelia hurtled along it,
the thump and scrape of the Beast's
uneven stride echoing behind them.
Finally, the tunnel opened into an
almost spherical chamber, its curved
walls sparkling with jagged crystals.
Huge pillar-like shards of diamond
reached almost to the ceiling. A
single shaft of sunlight pierced the
crystal cave, making a section of the

floor glow like a splintered rainbow trapped in ice.

Despite the chamber's astonishing beauty, Tom's stomach sank. "We're trapped," he said. He looked at the sunlight pouring through the ceiling and clenched his teeth. The slanting ray would be more than enough to restore Karixa's powers.

"Take cover!" Amelia cried, pointing to a glittering pillar. Tom, Elenna and Amelia leapt for shelter, just as Karixa burst into the cavern, striking the wall with her mighty blade.

CRASH! A hail of needle-sharp diamond splinters chimed against the walls and floor. Tom glanced from behind the pillar to see Karixa turning her head slowly from side to side, her massive shoulders low and her diamond sword lifted before her.

Finally, Karixa's hungry eyes fell on the pillar that hid the three intruders. Tom shuddered as the faintest smile traced her lips.

"Get behind me!" he shouted to Amelia and Elenna. Karixa bent her knees and pounced, shattering the pillar with one blow of her sword.

Tom threw his shield up to protect Amelia and Elenna from the lethal shards slicing towards them. Chunks of crystal thudded against the wood, almost buckling his arm, and the clatter of falling diamonds filled

the air. When the din fell silent, Tom
glanced from behind his shield.
Karixa had vanished.

"She's gone!" Amelia cried.

"No," Tom said, his spine tingling

as if charged with static. *Even without the red jewel of Torgor I know when I'm being watched!* He scanned the diamond walls. "I can feel her presence. She's camouflaged herself. This is just a game to her. We're the prize."

Tom, Amelia and Elenna shuffled backwards until they reached the sharp-toothed spikes of the chamber wall. Tom kept his sword and shield raised before them, glancing about for any sign of the Beast.

"Now what?" Amelia whispered.

"Do you think you can reach any loose chips of diamond?" Elenna asked.

"It's too dangerous!"Tom hissed.

But Amelia had already lunged from the cover of his shield. She dashed across the cave, scooped up a handful of shards, then turned to scramble back.

"Hurry!"Tom cried. At the same moment, Karixa morphed from the cover of a towering pillar and leapt right into Amelia's path. *No!* Amelia's eyes shot wide with alarm. She lifted her hand and threw her diamond chips towards Elenna, just as Karixa slammed a huge fist into her chest. Amelia shot across the room and crumpled to the ground, doubled over. Tom could hear Amelia wheezing and gasping for breath as

Karixa stalked towards her. *She's alive! I have to help her!* The beam of sunlight piercing the chamber roof hit the crystal floor just paces from Amelia's huddled form. Karixa stepped into the golden shaft, and lifted her arms.

Tom stared, horrified, his mind scrabbling for a plan, as Karixa drew light into her body. Still bent double, Amelia looked up at the Beast, her eyes shining with fear. The air hissed and crackled. Soon the pulsing light in Karixa's chest lit the chamber as bright as day. The Beast stepped towards Amelia's cowering form.

She'll be burned to a crisp! Tom ran out, hardly knowing what he planned to do, dimly aware of Elenna checking the tension of her bowstring, preparing to fire. He dived past Karixa, threw himself before Amelia, and lifted his shield.

Crack! A tremendous flash filled the cave. A wave of heat hit Tom,

so powerful he felt the skin on his face start to blister. The shield in his hand burst into a hungry mass of crackling yellow flames, and the sound of Beastly laugher echoed around him.

7

STEEL VS DIAMOND

Tom gritted his teeth and gripped his blazing shield, protecting Amelia from Karixa's power. Within moments he felt the searing heat blistering his hands and arms, but he held the shield steady. The flames licked at his tunic. The pain became almost unbearable. Finally, the light in Karixa's eyes faded. Tom threw the flaming wood aside and lifted his sword. Karixa glared down at him, her body no longer glowing. But Tom knew that her power would return, very soon. From the corner of his eye, Tom could see Elenna fiddling with her arrows.

"What are you doing?" he called.

"Just keep her distracted!" Elenna shouted.

That's about all I can do! Tom thought. Deep in the back of his mind, a terrible idea was taking shape. *This Beast is too much for us.* But Tom tightened his grip on his sword. *While there's blood in my veins, I won't give up!*

He launched himself at the Beast, sending his sword slicing towards her massive chest. Karixa stepped back out of range and swung her fist. Tom was ready. He ducked beneath Karixa's arm and cannoned shoulder-first into her injured leg. *Crunch!* Tom felt a sharp pain as something in his shoulder gave way, but Karixa staggered and almost fell, big arms flailing. Tom leapt aside and readied himself for the Beast's next attack.

Karixa turned and fixed Tom with her glowing eyes. Her huge blade glittered as it swished towards Tom's face. Tom lifted his sword to block the blow.

Smash! Pain jolted along Tom's
arm from his fingers to his shoulder.
Somehow he managed to keep hold
of his weapon, but his arm, half
numb, half burning with agony,
wouldn't lift the blade. Karixa

circled, and Tom swallowed hard. From the corner of his eye he saw Elenna fit an arrow to her bow, and felt more defeated than ever. He knew Elenna could distract the Beast for a moment but, in the end, their weapons were useless against diamond. In the shadows beyond the Beast, Amelia dragged herself to her knees, but then doubled over again in pain. *We're finished!*

Elenna let her arrow fly.

CRACK! The shaft punched into Karixa's shoulder with a sound like splitting ice, and stuck there.

The Beast lifted her head and roared with pain. Tom stared in amazement.

Thwack! Another of Elenna's arrows smashed into Karixa's back beside the first.

Karixa turned and staggered towards Elenna, slashing the air with her sword.

A third arrow struck Karixa in the chest and lodged there. The Beast shook her massive head in a roar of agony and rage. Elenna sprinted past the diamond warrior to Tom's side.

"But how?" Tom asked.

Elenna grinned and held up an arrow. The tip glittered with rainbow light.

Of course! Tom thought. *Only diamond can pierce diamond!* Karixa's weakness.

Tom had a sudden idea.

"Elenna!" Tom said. "This might sound crazy, but we need to get Karixa to harvest more light. A lot of light."

Elenna frowned. "That does sound crazy. The light makes her stronger!"

"Trust me," Tom said.

Karixa was already crossing the room with massive strides, heading towards the source of her power shining from above. Tom and Elenna watched as the Beast stood in the shaft of light and lifted her arms. She drew the energy into herself, magnifying it, letting it build to a bright pulsing ball of white light in her chest. The crackle and sizzle of scorched air filled the cave, along with a dazzling brightness like the midday sun. Finally, the Beast let her massive arms fall and turned her deadly gaze on Tom.

Tom glanced at the weakened sword in his aching hand and took a deep breath. I hope this works!

Crack! A bolt of pure white light lanced towards Tom's heart. Tom lifted his sword, tilting the blade to what his trained muscles knew must be just the right angle...

The beam struck the flat of Tom's blade and glanced back towards the Beast. It hit Karixa squarely in the chest, right where the shaft of Elenna's arrow still pierced the diamond flesh. The smile of victory on Karixa lips vanished in an instant. Her glowing eyes opened wide in a look of outraged surprise. Then, with a sound like a

thousand mirrors breaking at once, tiny glowing cracks spread outwards from the wound in Karixa's chest. Soon her whole body crackled with energy.

Karixa fixed her eyes on Tom and tipped her head in the briefest of nods. Then her massive body collapsed in a cascade of glittering crystals. Tom watched the diamonds fall, poised on the balls of his feet, his sword raised ready to strike if Karixa should re-form. At last, the sound of clattering crystals echoed to silence. The huge pile of diamonds settled, and fell still. Tom let his breath out in a long sigh of relief. The final Beast was defeated!

THE WAY HOME

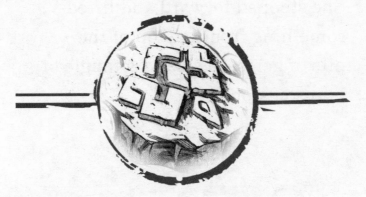

Tom and Elenna stepped towards
the mound of diamonds shining
in the stream of golden light from
above. Amelia struggled to her feet
and hobbled to join them.

"That was quite a light show!"
she said, clapping Tom on the
back. Tom glanced at his opponent,
and saw that her smile was genuine.

He grinned back.

"Hey – what's that?" Amelia said.
She stepped forward and lifted
something from the top of the
pile of gems – a small rectangle of
crimson stone.

"I think this is yours," Amelia said, handing it to Tom.

Tom took the stone, and ran his thumb over a strange symbol etched into its surface.

"The Rune of Courage!" he said. "We've completed the trial!"

"And it looks as if our passage home is ready," Elenna said, pointing towards a shimmering crack in the cavern wall, opening before their eyes.

In moments, the crack stood as wide as a doorway. Beyond it, Tom could see wooden floorboards and part of a stone wall hung with a tapestry stitched in rich red and gold.

"King Hugo's throne room!" he cried.

As Tom readied himself to walk through, he felt a swell of pride at what they had achieved. He and Elenna were almost at the doorway

when he realised Amelia had held back. She was looking downwards, cheeks red with shame.

"What's the matter?" he asked.

"I don't deserve to return with you," she muttered. "Not after the

way I've behaved."

Tom put a hand on her shoulder. "We wouldn't have completed the Quest without you," he said.

Amelia looked up at him, and managed half a smile.

Then they stepped through the portal together.

King Hugo's head snapped towards them as their boots touched the wooden boards. Aduro and Daltec, on either side of Hugo's throne, turned and stared. Tom held out his hand, showing them the red rune nestling in his palm. All three faces lit up with huge smiles.

"Greetings!" King Hugo boomed. "I am so glad to see you return!"

Daltec said. "But where is Dray?"

Tom glanced at Amelia, to see the colour drain from her face.

"It's a long story," Tom said. "I'll explain…"

When Tom had finished, Amelia stepped forwards, her shoulders square and her chin held high. "I understand now that Tom is Avantia's true Master of the Beasts," she said. "And I also see that I am unworthy of ever earning such a title."

"No!" Tom and Elenna said at once. "Like I told you," Tom added, "it took all of our efforts to complete this Quest!"

Daltec nodded. "Tom is right," he said. He looked at Amelia with a proud smile. "You set off on your Quest with less than noble intentions. However, you recognised you were on the wrong path, and fought hard to find the right one. Only a truly honourable hero is capable of that."

Amelia dropped her eyes to the floor, blushing red again. "Thank you," she said.

"You have lived up to your ancestor's legacy," Aduro said. "Which means you are ready to begin training to fulfil your destiny."

Amelia gaped at him. "What do you mean?"

"If you are willing," Aduro went on, "I plan to send you to Gwildor to train with Freya."

"Who is Freya?" Amelia asked.

Tom grinned. "My mother. She's Gwildor's Mistress of the Beasts. I think you'll like her."

Amelia took a deep breath and seemed to grow taller, her back straightening and her chin high. "I would be honoured!" she said at last.

"Well, that's settled then," King Hugo said from his throne. "Now, I can see you three young heroes all need medical care. And a good meal too, I expect." Tom's stomach grumbled as soon as he heard the words. "Please retire to your rooms," Hugo went on, "and I will have hot water sent up so you can bath."

"Ah! If I may, Your Majesty," Aduro

cut in. "I must borrow our three heroes for just a little longer." Aduro and Daltec crossed to a door at the back of the throne room. "Please follow me," Aduro said.

Tom, Elenna and Amelia followed Aduro and Daltec along corridors and down winding flights of stairs, until they reached a familiar, hidden doorway, far below the palace.

Daltec and Aduro led them inside. Torches flickered on the walls, casting dancing shadows over carved stone tombs.

Amelia stared around the dusky chamber, her eyes wide. "What is this place?" she asked.

"The Gallery of Tombs," Daltec

answered. "The resting place of long-gone Beasts and heroes."

Aduro and Daltec led them through the silent, ancient vaults to a stone door Tom had never noticed before. Daltec rested his hand on the door and turned to Tom, Elenna and Amelia.

"Inside here you will find every rune recovered from the Trial of Heroes," he said. Then he pushed the door and gestured inside.

Tom stepped past Daltec into the room. He glanced about, then looked back at Daltec with a frown.

"Is this a joke?" he said.

Daltec shook his head. Tom stepped further into the room,

followed by Elenna and Amelia. They all stared around the small oval space, then looked at each other in confusion. A deep ledge, perfect for storing precious artefacts, ran all the way around the wall. But apart from a single broadsword at one end, it was empty.

Daltec and Aduro stepped into the room. Tom turned to them. "I don't understand," he said. Daltec flashed him a sheepish smile.

Aduro spread his hands. "Only one warrior has ever returned from the Trial of Heroes," he said. "We thought it best not to mention this before you set out, in case the

knowledge caused you to lose heart."

Amelia gasped. Tom felt the cold
silence of the tomb press closer
about him as he took in the meaning
of Aduro's words. *Almost no one
has ever survived the trial...* He

turned to Elenna and she met
his look, her mouth wide open
with shock. Then Elenna grinned
suddenly, and punched Tom on
the shoulder. "Clearly, none of the
other questers had such a brave and

resourceful best friend then!"
she said.

Tom laughed. "You're right," he
replied, placing the Rune of Courage
on the shelf. "Here's to many more
Beast Quests!"

THE END

CONGRATULATIONS, YOU HAVE COMPLETED THIS QUEST!

At the end of each chapter you were awarded a special gold coin. The QUEST in this book was worth an amazing 8 coins.

Look at the Beast Quest totem picture inside the back cover of this book to see how far you've come in your journey to become

MASTER OF THE BEASTS.

The more books you read, the more coins you will collect!

Do you want your own
Beast Quest Totem?
1. Cut out and collect the coin below
2. Go to the Beast Quest website
3. Download and print out your totem
4. Add your coin to the totem
www.beastquest.co.uk/totem

8

Don't miss the first exciting Beast Quest book in this series, KRYTOR THE BLOOD BAT!

Read on for a sneak peek...

HOME!

"Ouch!" Elenna yelped, hopping onto one foot. "I've got a stone in my boot!"

Tom grinned as he watched his friend retrieve the stone and hurl it away.

"Just a little pebble," he said, pleased to have a moment to rest. "I can't believe you're complaining so much. We've been through worse."

"A lot worse." Elenna laughed. "Why couldn't Daltec magic us back from Gwildor?"

She has a point, Tom thought. The journey back to Avantia had been long and gruelling, taking them over both land and sea.

Tom lifted his chin. Being a Master of the Beasts meant doing difficult things. This journey home was just part of that. He pointed up ahead at the soaring towers of King Hugo's palace in the City. "Look, not that far now."

"Then what are waiting for?" Elenna winced as she strode

forwards. "I really do need to get my boots mended. Right now, they have more holes than they do leather."

Tom smiled again, but it was forced. Elenna's footwear wasn't the only thing that needed mending. His fingers crept to the shield that hung from his side. It had not been the same since the Beast Thoron's lightning struck it. The battle-scarred wood was rough beneath his fingertips, and the tokens that studded the shield were cool to the touch. They had been drained of colour and their powers still had not returned.

"I'm sure Aduro or Daltec will be able to fix your shield," Elenna said, watching Tom closely.

"I hope so," Tom murmured.

"What are you looking forward to most about being home?" Elenna asked after a moment.

Tom could tell that she was trying to take his mind off things.

"A warm bath," Tom said. "And a soft bed. It will be nice to sleep and not worry about being on a Quest just for—"

"Wait, can you smell that?" Elenna interrupted. "It's smoke."

Tom sniffed. His friend was right. He ran forward, taking the twisty road at a sprint. *People might be in danger!*

Tom and Elenna rounded the bend

and were faced with the remains of a
charred wagon on the road. Its cover
was completely scorched and the
wheels were just blackened stumps.

Crates, upturned baskets and rotting fruit and vegetables were strewn over the road but there didn't appear to be any people in sight.

Elenna poked at a charred apple with her toe. "Looks like some market traders were on the way to the City when the wagon caught fire."

"There are no wounded or dead, though," Tom said. "Everyone escaped."

He continued to scan the scene of the accident. There were scorch-marks up and down the path but they appeared as patches rather than as a trail of fire. *How odd. How did the fire start in the first place?* he wondered. *And why was it allowed to do so much damage without someone trying to stop it?*

Tom looked further up the path and saw more patches of ash on the ground, with swathes of vegetation burned away on either side. "Elenna, something is not right about this."

His friend nodded. "Let's get to the City. We might get some answers there."

They quickened their pace, and soon arrived at the city gates.

"Halt!" a soldier at the entrance said.

"Greetings. I am Tom, Master of the Beasts and protector of Avant—"

The soldier snorted. "I know who you are."

Tom paused. He wasn't expecting a great fanfare. After all, news probably hadn't come yet from Gwildor of their successes in the previous Quests. Still, he normally got along with Captain Harkman's troops.

Tom looked at the other soldiers on the gate. They were all scowling at him.

"Do we have a problem here?" Elenna asked, hands on hips.

"I'd say so." The first soldier waved them towards the gate irritably. "It's way past time the Master of the Beasts turned up."

Tom frowned as they turned grudgingly to open the gates. The soldier seemed angry at him. But why?

As the gates swung open, a flurry of red and orange filled his vision. It was Epos the Flame Bird, in the middle of the courtyard beyond! The Good Beast was in chains, thrashing on the ground. A manacle encircled her long elegant neck and steel chains bound her mighty wings.

Tom ran forward and drew his sword ready to sever her bonds. As he did so, Epos let out a pitiful keen, almost as if she was scared of him.

Tom lowered his sword, anger making him shake. *Poor Epos*, he thought as he approached her. *She no longer knows who is friend or foe.*

Elenna was running right by his side, her face determined. As they got

nearer to Epos, a throng of soldiers
formed ranks around the flame bird.

"Let me through," Tom demanded.
"I'm Master of the Beasts."

"No one is to go near the Beast

under pain of death," one of the
soldiers said. "King Hugo's orders."
Tom's fingers tightened on his
sword but Elenna shook her head.
"Fighting is not the answer," she

said. "We should speak to King Hugo and find out what's going on."

Tom nodded but, first, he wanted to hear what Epos had to say. He sheathed his sword, then called on the power of his red jewel and tried to form a connection with the Beast. But all he could sense was confusion.

I'll come back for you, Epos, Tom vowed. *Right after I get some answers.*

Read
KRYTOR THE BLOOD BAT
to find out what happens next!

FIGHT THE BEASTS,
FEAR THE MAGIC

Are you a BEAST QUEST mega fan?
Do you want to know about all the latest news,
competitions and books before anyone else?

Then join our Quest Club!

Visit the BEAST QUEST website
and sign up today!

www.beastquest.co.uk

Discover the new Beast Quest mobile game from

Available free on iOS and Android

Available on **iTunes**   GET IT ON **Google play**   **amazon**.com

Guide Tom on his Quest to free the Good Beasts
of Avantia from Malvel's evil spells.

Battle the Beasts, defeat the minions,
unearth the secrets and collect
rewards as you journey through the
Kingdom of Avantia.

31901064428313

DOWNLOAD THE APP TO BEGIN
THE ADVENTURE NOW!